Amber Stewart ✷ Layn Marlow ✷ Sheryl Webster ✷ Tim Warnes ✷ Charlotte Middleton ✷ Jan Ormerod ✷ Lindsey Gardiner

Shall We Share A Story Tonight?

OXFORD
UNIVERSITY PRESS

OXFORD
UNIVERSITY PRESS

Great Clarendon Street, Oxford OX2 6DP

Oxford University Press is a department of the University of Oxford.
It furthers the University's objective of excellence in research,
scholarship, and education by publishing worldwide in

Oxford   New York

Auckland   Cape Town   Dar es Salaam   Hong Kong   Karachi
Kuala Lumpur   Madrid   Melbourne   Mexico City   Nairobi
New Delhi   Shanghai   Taipei   Toronto

With offices in
Argentina   Austria   Brazil   Chile   Czech Republic   France   Greece
Guatemala   Hungary   Italy   Japan   Poland   Portugal   Singapore
South Korea   Switzerland   Thailand   Turkey   Ukraine   Vietnam

Oxford is a registered trade mark of Oxford University Press
in the UK and in certain other countries

This edition first published in 2013
Just Like Tonight first published in 2009
What Small Rabbit Heard first published in 2010
Christopher Nibble first published in 2009
Whoosh Around the Mulberry Bush first published in 2007

British Library Cataloguing in Publication Data
Data available

ISBN: 978-0-19-273390-0 (hardback)

2 4 6 8 10 9 7 5 3 1

Printed in China

Paper used in the production of this book is a natural,
recyclable product made from wood grown in sustainable forests.
The manufacturing process conforms to the environmental
regulations of the country of origin.

Contents

Amber Stewart & Layn Marlow

Just Like Tonight

It was bedtime for Button.

'My little bear cub must be tired,' said Mummy,
'after such a busy day.'
'Sweet dreams,' said Daddy.

As they kissed him goodnight,
Button thought sleepily about his day
and wondered what his dreams might bring.

He remembered lazing in the
early morning sunshine . . .

climbing with his
big sisters . . .

playing by their
favourite pool . . .

and finding
interesting insects,

even a ladybird with three spots on one wing and not
a single spot on the other. Button found it on the fallen
tree that looked like a big bear asleep in the grass.

Button had forgotten about the
big, scary tree-bear until that very moment.
Supposing it came into his dreams tonight?

He couldn't take the risk.

'Mummy! Daddy!' he called.

Button told them all about his scary tree-bear worry.

Daddy said, 'Shall I give you
something nice to think about
before you go to sleep?
Nice thoughts always keep
the bad ones away.'

'Yes please,' Button nodded,
feeling much braver about
the scary tree-bear already.

'Well,' wondered Daddy, 'shall I tell you about
a day when there were no scary things?
A day *so* happy that if you think of it tonight
only sweet dreams will come.'

'What day was that, Daddy?' asked Button.
Daddy kissed the top of his nose and said,
'The day you were born . . .'

'It was one of those days that started misty, but I knew
a hot and sunny day was just around the corner.'

'A bit like today?' asked Button.
'When I woke up I couldn't even
see over the berry bush!'

'Yes, just like today,' Daddy smiled, 'and on the day you were born, I gathered the juiciest berries and stickiest honey.'

'A bit like today?' asked Button,
as he remembered lying in the
warm sun eating his sweet
breakfast berries.

'Yes,' said Daddy, 'but even more delicious.'

'On the day you were born,'
Daddy continued, 'your big sisters were so
happy they found special presents for you . . .'

'Like my lucky pine-cone,' said Button,
'and my little log-boat! And did they want
to play with me too?'

'Oh yes!' laughed Daddy. 'They wanted to play
with you right there and then, but Mummy
said you needed to grow a little first . . .'

'And now I've grown!' said
Button. 'We played so much
today we had to jump in
Two Rivers Pool to cool down.'

'When evening came,' remembered Daddy,
'I took you in my arms to watch your
first-ever sunset and sing you a lullaby.'

'Just like *every* evening,' yawned Button.
He loved watching the sun go down with Daddy
and singing songs that made them laugh.

'And on your very first night,' said Daddy quietly, 'you were so tired you fell fast asleep. Mummy and I watched over you, and no scary tree-bear and bad dreams came to disturb our little one.'

'Just like tonight?' said Button.
'Yes,' whispered Daddy.

And Daddy was right . . .
only sweet dreams came.

What Small

Rabbit heard

Sheryl Webster
Tim Warnes

Small Rabbit did not
want to go for a walk.

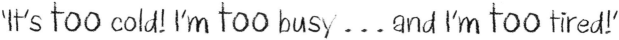

'It's too cold! I'm too busy ... and I'm too tired!'

'It's not cold, it's **fresh**,' said Big Rabbit.
'You're not busy, you're **playing**.
And you are certainly **not yet tired!**'

'Well, it's **too** windy. It won't be fun.'

'Of course it will be fun,' said Big Rabbit. **'Now off we go.'**

Outside the wind howled.

Whooooo!

Small Rabbit
began to
hop and skip
to keep
himself warm.

Big Rabbit wanted Small Rabbit
to stay close.

'Try to keep up,' she said.
But Big Rabbit's words were
lost in the howl of the wind.

What Small Rabbit
heard was . . .

'Jump in the mud..'

So he did.

The wind howled. *Whooooo!*
It picked up a pile of leaves
and they danced past Small Rabbit.

He began to chase them.
Big Rabbit shivered
and shouted,
'Stay with me, please.'

Again her words were
lost in the howl of the wind.

What Small Rabbit
heard was . . .

'Roll in the leaves.'
So he did!

Soon they came to Thistledown Field.

'Yippee!' yelled Small Rabbit, pointing to the animals.
Big Rabbit called to Small Rabbit
as she tried to catch up,

'I want you to wait!'

The wind howled.  Whooooo!

PLEASE SHUT
THE GATE

What Small Rabbit heard was . . .

'Open the gate.'
So he did!

Small Rabbit raced up the hill.
It was getting colder and his
coat flapped in the wind as he ran.

Big Rabbit was still trying to close the gate but she cried out, 'Fasten your coat.'

The wind howled.

Whooooo!

What Small Rabbit heard was . . .

'Ride on the goat.'
So he did . . .

all the way to the top of the hill!

Big Rabbit was worried that Small Rabbit
might get blown off the top, and she
shouted as loudly as she could,

'Keep very still.'

But it was her words that were blown away.
What Small Rabbit heard was . . .

'Roll down
the hill.'
So he did.

Big Rabbit was quite out of
puff and she could think of only
one way to catch up.

She shouted as she rolled,

'Wait for meeeee!'

The wind howled
all around.

What Small Rabbit
heard was . . .

'Climb the treeeee.'
So he did.

Small Rabbit swung from a branch.
Suddenly, he spotted his rabbit
hole on the other side of the
stream and he started
to hop home.

A thought flashed through Big Rabbit's mind.
She looked at how dirty Small Rabbit was.
She thought of their lovely clean burrow.

'Small Rabbit, don't go inside!' she pleaded.

The wind howled.
Whooooo!

Big Rabbit peeked cautiously into the burrow.
She tiptoed in.

It was quiet. Too quiet.

Very slowly, she opened the cupboard door.

'Boo!'

laughed Small Rabbit.
'It took me ages to find somewhere to hide.

But I did!'

Small Rabbit leapt into Big Rabbit's arms.
'Windy walks are lots and lots of fun!' he said.

And Big Rabbit had to agree.

CHARLOTTE MIDDLETON

presents

CHRISTOPHER Nibble

in a tale of dandelion derring-do!

If there was one thing Christopher Nibble **loved** more than football,

it was . . .

eating dandelion leaves.

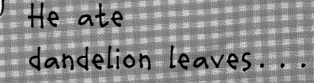

He ate
dandelion leaves. . .

at breakfast
time,

at lunch
time,

and at
dinner time.

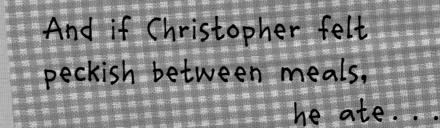

And if Christopher felt
peckish between meals,
he ate. . .

MORE dandelion leaves!
But it was not just Christopher who liked
dandelion leaves. Mr and Mrs Nibble liked them.
His sister liked them. His friends liked them.

In fact . . . every guinea pig
in Dandeville **loved** dandelion leaves.

munch

munch

nibble

munch

nibble

All day long the happy
sound of munching and
nibbling filled the air . . .

until, that is, dandelion leaves began to run out.

Dandelion dishes were taken off the menus, and dandelion drinks disappeared from the shelves.

Menu Today

Carrot and lettuce wrap on a bed of ~~dandelion~~ leaves cabbage

~~Dandelion~~ soup cabbage

cabbage ~~Dandelion~~ and broccoli quiche

~~Dandelion~~ juice sold out

The last few leaves could be bought
on the internet...

for a HUGE amount of money!

Soon the worst thing imaginable happened...

all over town the dandelions had been
munched to nothing more than bitten-down
stalks, and the guinea pigs had to make do...

with chewy cabbage instead!

Just one dandelion was left but nobody knew about it, except Christopher Nibble. It happened to be growing right outside his bedroom window.

Christopher's mouth
watered at the sight of it.
But he knew he mustn't eat it,
or let anyone else eat it,
not if it was the last dandelion in town.

It might even be the last dandelion
in the whole world!
He thought hard and decided . . .

... to go to
the library.

He borrowed a book called
'Everything You Need to
Know about Dandelions'

Bugs

THE
WAY OF THE
BUG

The BIG
GRUB
Book

SUPER SNAILS
The Wonderful World of Words

and he read it very carefully.

He found a little
cloche to protect
his dandelion. . .

and every day he
watered it and
picked off the bugs.

Every day he was very good about not taking even the tiniest little nibble while he . . .

waited,
and waited,
and waited.

Until, finally, his dandelion had grown the most beautiful white head of tiny seeds.

Very gently,
Christopher picked it
and carried it all
the way up
Daisy Chain Hill.
When he reached
the top...

he had just
enough puff to take
a deep breath and...

and landed gently all over Dandeville.

At first nobody noticed.

But soon the new
plants started to sprout
fresh leaves.

And in no time at all Dandeville
was filled with the happy sound
of munching once more.

As for Christopher,

But now

there's

something

he loves just

as much

as eating

dandelions. . . .

Christopher loves **GROWING** them!

THIS book takes its inspiration from the much-loved song 'Here We Go Round the Mulberry Bush': the words can be sung to the same rhythm and there are animal noises and actions, too. It's a book that invites lots of high-energy enjoyment but it's also a book that can be shared with young children to talk about habitats around the world, encouraging them to develop an awareness of the great diversity of wildlife that our planet supports. The book begins with animals you might find in a garden or on a farm. There are also animals from seashore, ocean, desert, rainforest, savannah, arctic and wetland habitats and the book finishes with a group of nocturnal animals in a night-time setting.

Whoosh around the Mulberry Bush

Jan
Ormerod

Lindsey
Gardiner

Here we go round the mulberry bush,

with a mulberry whoosh and a mulberry swoosh.

Here we go round the mulberry bush on a **COLD** and **frosty** morning.

This is the way we slime along,
flippety flap and sing a song.

Here we go round the **flower bed** on a sweetly smelling morning.

Here we go round the **chicken coop** so early in the morning.

This is the way we **dig** and **dive**,
scuttle and **crawl**, **nip** and **pinch**.

Here we go round the **sandy shore** on a breezy summer morning.

This is the way we **flip** our fins,
swim and **swoop**,
dart and **dive**.

Here we go round the **deep** blue sea
on a **salty bubbly** morning.

Here we go round the

jungle vines

on a **hot** and

sticky

morning.

This is the way we **suck** and **slurp**, **wallow** in mud, **kick** our heels.

Here we go round the on a **dry** and **dusty** waterhole morning.

This is the way we slap and clap, slip and slide, splish and splash.

Here we go round the **icicle** on a **sparkling** snowy morning.

This is the way we Croaky Croak,
leap and jump, hop and flop.

Here we go round the mossy log on a misty moisty morning.

This is the way we **flit** and **fly**, **swoop** and **soar**, big eyes wide.

Here we go round the
starry night
just before the morning.